DARWIN
AND THE
ENCHANTED ISLES

DARWIN
AND THE
ENCHANTED ISLES

by Irwin Shapiro
illustrated by Christopher Spollen

Coward, McCann & Geoghegan, Inc./New York

ISBN 0-698-30679-1 lib. bdg.

Library of Congress Cataloging in Publication Data.

Shapiro, Irwin, 1911- Darwin and the enchanted isles. (A Science Discovery book) Bibliography: p.
SUMMARY: Describes the events leading to Darwin's voyage on the *Beagle* and the subsequent theories on evolution he posed based mainly on observations made on the Galapagos Islands.
1. Darwin, Charles Robert, 1809-1882—Juvenile Literature. 2. Evolution—History—Juvenile literature. 3. Naturalists—England—Biography—Juvenile literature. [1. Darwin, Charles Robert, 1809-1882. 2. Naturalists. 3. Evolution—History] I. Spollen, Christopher J. II. Title. QH31.D2S5 575'.0092'4 [B] [92] 77-7544

DARWIN
AND THE
ENCHANTED ISLES

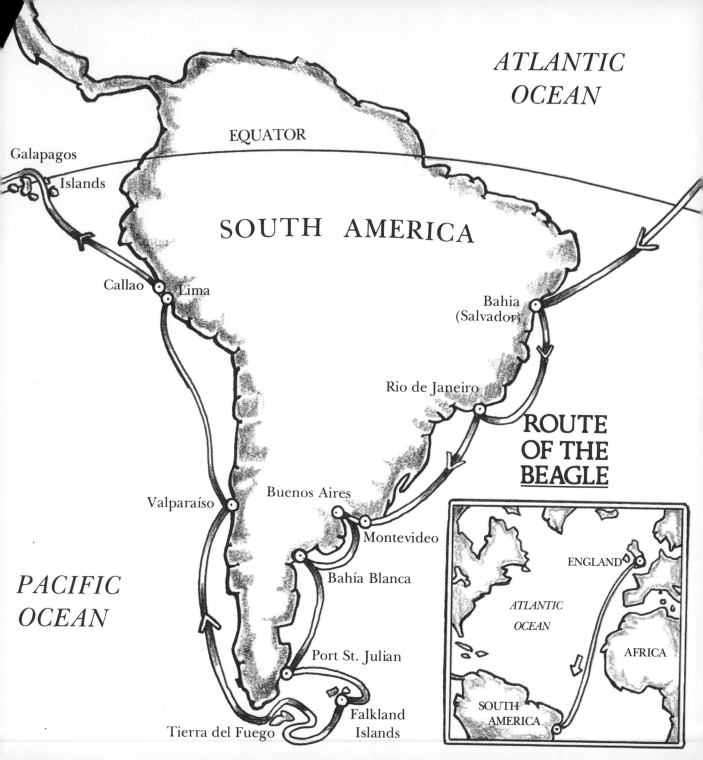

ATLANTIC
OCEAN

EQUATOR

Galapagos
Islands

SOUTH AMERICA

Callao Lima

Bahia
(Salvador)

Rio de Janeiro

**ROUTE
OF THE
BEAGLE**

Valparaíso   Buenos Aires

PACIFIC
OCEAN

Montevideo

Bahía Blanca

Port St. Julian

Tierra del Fuego

Falkland
Islands

ENGLAND

ATLANTIC
OCEAN

AFRICA

SOUTH
AMERICA

CONTENTS

1 / THE ISLANDS, THE BOY, THE MAN

THE ENCANTADAS

In the Pacific Ocean, touching the equator, lies a group of strange islands. Six hundred miles east is South America, a thousand miles northeast the Panama Canal—and yet these islands might be on another planet. Nowhere else on earth is there anything like them.

Volcanoes made the islands, pouring out burning hot lava from beneath the sea. The lava piled up, cooled, and hardened into rock. The newly made land was formed into plains, mounds, hills, and volcanic craters. Some of the craters were small cones; others were huge and taller than four thousand feet.

Only the high slopes, watered by heavy clouds, became green with plants. On the low plains rain seldom fell. Little grew besides cactus and scrubby bushes. The fields of twisted, tumbled rock were black, as if scorched by fire.

But over the centuries birds settled on the islands—land birds and sea birds, hawks, finches, mockingbirds, frigate birds, gulls, boobies. With the birds appeared monsters. At least, they had the look of monsters; they were mild in manner and lived peacefully enough with their neighbors. There were slimy lizards, like miniature dragons or dinosaurs, and tortoises, giant tortoises, dragging slowly about like creatures in a dream.

So it was that the Spaniards, who discovered the islands, called them the Galapagos, or Tortoise Islands. They also called them the Encantadas, or Enchanted Isles. They felt a strangeness in these lonely islands and their creatures, a secret, a mystery they could not understand. Truly these bits of land in the sea seemed under a magic spell.

Enchanted or not, the Galapagos became a hideout for pirates. They knew that on these out-of-the-way islands they were safe from capture. They could rest and count their loot before sailing off again.

Years later, sailors from whaling ships stopped here to catch tortoises for fresh meat. They said this was a place for devils, that it looked much like hell. As for the tortoises, they were cruel ship captains who had died and had been changed into tortoises for their sins.

Meanwhile, on another island thousands of miles away, a boy named Charles Robert Darwin was growing up. In time, he would break the enchantment of the Galapagos. He would discover their secret, he would solve their mystery. When he did, he would shock the world and change its thinking.

And, curiously, Darwin came to the Galapagos almost by accident. He almost never saw the Galapagos at all—first, because of his father, and then because of his nose.

SHOOTING, DOGS, AND RAT-CATCHING

Charles Darwin was born in England on February 12, 1809, the same day as Abraham Lincoln. His mother died when he was eight years old, and he was brought up by his sisters. But the real ruler of the big house in Shrewsbury was his father, Dr. Robert Darwin.

Dr. Darwin was a huge man. He weighed more than three hundred pounds and was over six feet tall. When he came home, one of his daughters said, it was like the tide rolling in. Often he would gather his children around him and talk to them for two hours at a time. Standing before him, Charles felt small and a little frightened. But Dr. Darwin was also a kind and generous man, and Charles would have liked to please him.

It was not easy. No matter how he tried, Charles never did well in school. Mathematics, Latin, Greek—he hated them all. They meant nothing to him; what interested him was the world outside the classroom. He loved dogs, horses, and everything in nature. He enjoyed fishing and going on long walks. More than anything else, he loved to collect things. He collected plants, rocks, coins, butterflies, insects, birds' eggs. With his older brother, Erasmus, he did chemistry experiments in the family toolshed, and his schoolmates called him "Gas."

"The school as a means of education to me was simply a blank," he said years later. "I learned absolutely nothing except by amusing myself reading and experimenting in chemistry." His teachers thought him "a very ordinary boy," not as bright as most.

At the age of fifteen Charles learned to ride, shoot, and hunt. He became an expert shot, and shooting game birds was one of the most important things in his life. Watching him rush off to hunt, watching him fill his room with cases of his collections, his father was not pleased.

"You care for nothing but shooting, dogs, and rat-catching," Dr. Darwin said angrily, "and you will be a disgrace to yourself and your family."

Staring at his son, Dr. Darwin slowly shook his head. No, it would not do. After all, the Darwins were a well-known family. Dr. Darwin was a successful and highly respected physician, as his father had been before him. Charles's mother was one of the Wedgwoods, also a well-known family. Her brother, Josiah, Charles's Uncle Jos, was the head of a pottery factory famous throughout the world. No, thought Dr. Darwin, he could not allow Charles to disgrace them all.

True, the Darwins had enough money so that Charles need

never work for a living. Even so, he must make something of himself. He must be a doctor, like his father and grandfather.

"I have decided," Dr. Darwin said. Charles would go to Edinburgh in Scotland and study medicine.

"Yes, Father," said Charles.

THE MAN WHO WALKS WITH HENSLOW

In Edinburgh, Charles soon found that the lectures on medicine almost put him to sleep. The second time he watched an operation, he ran out of the room. Such pain-killing drugs as chloroform and ether were not yet in use, and as he ran he could hear the screams of the patient.

Charles could not stand the sight of suffering; he could not even stand the sight of blood. He never watched an operation again. He stayed on at medical school to please his father, but he knew he could never be a doctor.

Again, it was the world outside the classroom that interested him. He went on collecting, and began to learn something of geology. From a black man who had been on an expedition to South America he learned to stuff and mount birds. He attended meetings of people who, like himself, were interested in the study of nature, of plants and animals and insects. This branch of science was called natural history, and the scientists in this field were called naturalists. But Charles had no idea of becoming a naturalist; his nature studies were simply a hobby.

14

In two years he was back home in Shrewsbury. Dr. Darwin sighed. He agreed that Charles could never be a doctor. On the other hand, he could not be just an idle sportsman. He could not spend his life riding and shooting and making endless collections. He must have a career of some kind. But what? Well, Charles could do what many another rich young man of no particular ability did. He could go into the Church and be a minister. He could be a country parson, if nothing else.

Although Charles was not especially religious, he had been raised in the Church of England and believed every word in the Bible. He had no great wish to be a minister, but he had nothing against it, either. There were worse things than being a country parson. He could still go on collecting, he could still study nature, he could still ride and hunt, and it would all be pleasant enough.

"Yes, Father," Charles said.

And off he went to Cambridge University, to prepare for a career in the Church. He was nineteen years old and, in his own words, "as ignorant as a pig." He liked everything about Cambridge except his studies, and he spent as little time as possible on them. He went riding and hunting. He went to parties with his friends, and he did a little drinking and card-playing.

And he still collected. At Cambridge he became interested in beetles, and his room was filled with cases of specimens. He became friendly with Adam Sedgwick, Professor of Geology, and with John Stevens Henslow, Professor of Botany. He learned a great deal from them, about biology as well as geology and botany. He and Henslow often went on long nature walks together, and Charles became known as "the man who walks with Henslow."

From his talks with Henslow and Sedgwick, from his reading, from his collecting, he was learning more and more about natural history. He was learning how to observe, how to study plants and animals and insects. Without realizing it, without meaning to, he was training himself to be a naturalist.

But Charles still thought of his nature studies as a hobby. They were merely something he enjoyed, as he enjoyed riding and shooting.

"At that time," he said, "I should have thought myself mad to give up the first days of partridge-shooting for geology or any other science."

Besides, he had set out to become a minister, and a minister he would be—if he passed his final examinations. When he found out that he had indeed passed, he said, "I'm through, through, through!"

With college behind him, he could now begin his career in the Church. But he was in no hurry. There were other things he wanted to do first. He had read a book by Alexander von Humboldt, a famous naturalist and traveler, which described the wonders of the tropical rain forest. It made Charles want to visit strange places and see these wonders for himself. He planned a trip to the Canary Islands and learned Spanish.

From Cambridge he went on a trip to North Wales with Sedgwick. They wandered about the countryside for several

16

weeks, studying rock formations. Then Charles rushed back to Shrewsbury. The hunting season was about to begin, and he could hardly wait to get his hands on a gun.

When he reached home, he found a letter waiting for him—the letter that was to change his life. It was from Professor Henslow.

A WILD SCHEME

The British navy, Henslow wrote, was sending the ship *Beagle* on a scientific expedition around the world. Her chief mission was to survey and make charts of the coast of South America. She would be visiting lands still little known, and Captain Robert Fitzroy, her commander, was looking for a naturalist to go on the voyage. Henslow had recommended Charles Darwin. There would be no pay—in fact, Charles would have to pay his own expenses—but it was a great opportunity.

Charles smiled as he read and reread the letter. He knew it was the custom for expeditions like the *Beagle*'s to take along a naturalist. But he had never dreamed of making such a voyage himself; he had never even thought of himself as a real naturalist. And yet, Henslow had recommended him!

"I consider you to be the best-qualified person that I know of," Henslow wrote, " . . . for observing and noting anything worthy to be noted in Natural History . . . I think you are the very man they are in search of."

Charles smiled again. Yes, this was a great opportunity—

much better than a trip to the Canary Islands. Here was a chance to see the world, to visit strange places. Here was a chance to collect all sorts of rare specimens, to study new plants, new insects, new animals, new rock formations. What a grand adventure it would be!

First, of course, he had to get his father's permission. After all, he was still living on his father's money. Surely his father would not object; there was no reason why he should not go.

But when he went to talk to his father about it, he knew at once what the answer would be. The frown on Dr. Darwin's face, the way he sat in his chair, the way he looked at Charles—all said no.

After a moment of silence, Dr. Darwin spoke.

"This is a wild scheme," he said, pointing to the letter.

Charles had turned away from medicine; was he now turning away from the Church as well? The voyage would take at least two years. He would never settle down after that, he would no longer be thought fit to be a minister. How many times could he change his career? Besides, he would be far from comfortable on the cramped ship. The voyage might even be dangerous. And why had they asked Charles instead of someone better known? There was something wrong somewhere. The whole thing was senseless.

Dr. Darwin shook his head slowly.

"A wild scheme," he repeated. Then he said, "If you can find any man of common sense who advises you to go, I will give my consent."

"Yes, Father," said Charles.

A MAN OF COMMON SENSE

Returning to his room, Charles wrote a letter to Henslow. He would gladly have gone on the voyage of the *Beagle*. But his father was against it, and so he could not go.

Charles sighed. Oh, well . . . He could still go hunting, as he had planned—the partridge season was about to begin. And there was always good hunting on the grounds of Maer, his uncle Josiah Wedgwood's house, twenty miles away.

The next day he rode off to Maer. Uncle Jos was delighted to see him, as were his wife and daughters. When they heard of the offer to sail on the *Beagle,* they said, "Charles, you must accept."

"I cannot," Charles said, and told them of his father's objections.

"I believe that this time your father is wrong," Uncle Jos said. One by one he answered all of Dr. Darwin's objections. The study of natural history would certainly not make Charles unfit to be a minister. There was no need for him to change his profession. And why had Henslow recommended him? Plainly, because Henslow felt that Charles had the ability to be a fine naturalist. It was indeed a great opportunity.

Charles sent off a letter to his father, asking him to think about the matter again. Early the next morning he picked up his gun and went hunting. Uncle Jos sent a servant to call him back. This business of the *Beagle* was too important; they must see Dr. Darwin at once. They drove to the Darwins' house and soon were talking with Charles's father.

Yes, he had said he would consent if Charles could find any man of common sense who would advise him to go. Josiah Wedgwood was certainly a man of common sense. Dr. Darwin thought him the most sensible man he knew, and now he listened to him carefully.

Charles added that the expense would not be great.

"I should be deuced clever to spend more than my allowance whilst on the *Beagle*," he said.

Dr. Darwin smiled, remembering how much money Charles had spent at Cambridge.

"But they tell me you are very clever," he said quietly.

Even so, he gave his consent. But Charles was still not certain that he would sail on the *Beagle*. He had yet to meet Captain Fitzroy, the commander of the expedition. It was important for the two men to like each other. They would be thrown together for several years in the cramped quarters of a small ship.

For the sake of making the voyage, Charles was prepared to put up with almost anyone.

"But what will Captain Fitzroy think of me?" he wondered.

Less than a week later, he found out.

A SECOND LIFE

It was in London, after a hurried trip, that Charles first came face to face with Captain Fitzroy. The two young men—Charles was twenty-two, Fitzroy a little older—eyed each other. Charles immediately liked the handsome, serious naval officer.

"A spendid fellow," he thought. "Just the right man to lead the expedition."

Fitzroy was not so sure about Charles. He believed a man's character could be judged by his features, and he did not like the shape of Charles's nose. Could this Charles Darwin stand the hardships of a long voyage? According to his nose—no. It was the nose of someone who would break down, who would leave the ship before the voyage was over.

Fitzroy tried to warn Charles of what might lie ahead. But Charles was so eager, so willing, so cheerful, that Fitzroy changed his mind. In spite of that nose, the two men got along very well indeed. It was all settled—Charles would be the naturalist on the voyage of the *Beagle*.

Now Charles could hardly wait for the ship to sail.

He said, "My second life will then commence, and it shall be as a birthday for the rest of my life."

He made his preparations; he gathered his equipment. Among other things he bought a microscope, alcohol for preserving specimens, two pistols, and a rifle. He bought the pistols at Fitzroy's suggestion, to protect himself when he went ashore. The rifle he would use to shoot specimens of birds and animals, which he would then send to England, together with specimens of rocks, plants, and insects. There he and other scientists would be able to make a thorough study of them.

By the end of October he was in Plymouth, from whose port the *Beagle* was to sail. Charles had already said his good-byes in

Shrewsbury and Cambridge. He was ready for the voyage, more than ready. The trouble was, the ship was not ready. She needed repairs.

For two months, while the weather grew cold and gloomy, Charles could do little except wait. He kept going aboard the *Beagle*, rearranging his belongings in the cabin, and trying to look like a sailor. He did not think anyone was fooled.

He began to have pains around the heart. They were so bad that he feared he had heart disease. But he would not see a doctor. A doctor might tell him he was not fit for the voyage, and he was determined to go.

At last, on December 27, 1831, the ship sailed. His father had been right about one thing—his quarters were far from comfortable. The cabin was so small that he had to pull out the drawer of a locker to make room for his feet when he lay in his hammock. And he often had to lie down, for he suffered terribly from seasickness. All he could do was stretch out in his hammock; all he could eat was raisins.

His second life had commenced, his great adventure had begun—and he was miserable.

2 / ON THE <u>BEAGLE</u>

PHILOSOPHER AND FLYCATCHER

For the first weeks of the voyage, Charles could do little more than lie in his hammock and read. One of the books he read was *Principles of Geology* by Charles Lyell. It was a new book that Henslow had given him before he left.

"Read it by all means," Henslow said, "for it is very interesting, but do not pay any attention to it except in regard to facts, for it is altogether wild as far as theory goes."

Lyell's theory was that the earth had been changed in the past by earthquakes and volcanoes, by the action of glaciers and rivers, of wind and rain and snow. The earth was still changing, as its crust rose and sank, was heaved up or worn down, and it would go on changing in the future. The changes, however, were slow and gradual, and took millions of years.

Henslow, like almost all scientists of his day, believed that the changes had happened quickly and suddenly. They were brought about by catastrophes, like the flood spoken of in the Bible. God had created the earth, just as the Bible said, and only God could change it. And the earth was not nearly so old as Lyell thought. Some people even believed that Archbishop James Ussher had figured out the exact moment when the world had been created—at nine o'clock in the morning, on October 12, 4004 B.C.

Swaying in his hammock, Darwin thought: Who is right—Lyell or all the others? Well, he would test Lyell's theory. He would study the rock formations wherever he touched land. If only he weren't seasick! He wrote to his father, "The misery . . . is far beyond what I ever guessed at."

Luckily the ship stopped for twenty-three days at the Cape Verde Islands. As soon as he stepped on shore, he forgot his seasickness. He chipped off pieces of rock with a geologist's hammer and studied them under a magnifying glass. He looked closely at the birds and the trees. He made notes. He collected plants and insects which he would later ship to England. He was doing the work he had come for and was no longer miserable.

On the island of St. Jago he saw the first proof of Lyell's theory. Along the beach was a sea cliff, and on the cliff a band of white that went on for miles. He climbed up the cliff and peered at the band of white. It was made up of seashells embedded in rock—the same kind of shells he had found on the beach below.

26

How had the shells come to be here, so high above the beach?

There could be only one answer. The cliff had once been under the sea. Slowly, over thousands and thousands of years, the movements of the earth had made it rise out of the water. It seemed as though Lyell was right. His theory was not wild, after all. The earth had changed gradually. Could it still be changing?

As the *Beagle* went on toward Brazil, the sea became calmer. Darwin came out on deck, still wearing the clothes he had worn at home—long-tailed coat, waistcoat, and white shirt. The sailors looked at each other and smiled. They watched curiously as he threw a net over the side and drew up sea creatures to study. An officer complained that he was dirtying the clean deck with his haul. Darwin did not mind. He was doing his work. Nor did he mind when he heard the sailors call him the Philosopher and the Flycatcher.

In April the *Beagle* stopped at Rio de Janeiro, and he arranged to go on a hundred-mile trip through the rain forest.

Riding with six other men, observing everything about him, he was more and more delighted. He marveled at the palm trees, the brightly colored birds and butterflies, the flowers, the anthills, the monkeys. He was like a blind man, he said, who has just been given eyes and set down in a scene from the Arabian Nights.

That was to be the pattern of his life on the voyage—while Fitzroy surveyed and mapped the coast, Darwin went ashore and explored the land. Then the ship would pick him up at

some point for the next leg of the journey.

He sent case after case of the specimens he collected back to England—rocks, minerals, butterflies, spiders, crabs, plants, skins of birds and animals. Aboard the *Beagle* he experimented and studied his finds under his microscope. He no longer dreamed of hunting partridges; science was more exciting.

After a time he gave up shooting almost entirely. He hired Sims Covington, a young member of the crew, as his assistant. He had Covington shoot the birds and animals he wanted for specimens, and taught him how to stuff them. He wanted to be free to roam, to look, to observe, to study, to think.

He began to dress more like the sailors, and for a while he wore a beard. He wrote home that he looked like a half-washed chimney sweeper. At sea, whenever the weather was rough, he was still troubled by seasickness. But once on land he seemed able to stand any kind of hardship.

From Rio de Janeiro the *Beagle* sailed to Buenos Aires, and then 400 miles south to Bahia Blanca. This was a small settlement with a fort manned by Argentinian soldiers. They stared suspiciously at Darwin, who had two pistols in his belt and carried a geologist's hammer. They were even more suspicious when he began digging out some bones at Punta Alta, a cliff along the beach.

Darwin paid little attention to the soldiers. With Sims Covington, he dug away with a pickax. The two stayed the night, and he wrote in his journal, "Very successful with the bones, passed the night pleasantly."

When he hauled the bones aboard the ship, the sailors grinned.

"Look at the rubbish!" they said, and an officer called out, "You're dirtying the deck again with that damned stuff!"

Darwin shrugged. He knew he had made an important find. These fossilized bones were those of huge animals no longer on earth. Examining them, he found that some belonged to the Toxodon, which he described as like a hippopotamus and "one of the strangest animals ever discovered." The other bones were from a giant sloth, a giant armadillo, and a large guanaco, or wild llama. These last three were like animals that were still living, but much larger.

Why had the giant animals died out? Darwin knew what answer he would get from most people, even from scientists. They would say, "The giant animals were wiped out in a great catastrophe, like the flood at the time of Noah. Then God created the smaller animals."

Darwin found this hard to believe. There was no sign of a catastrophe great enough to wipe out all the giant animals. And if the smaller animals were created separately, why did they resemble the larger ones? Darwin's mind was filled with questions he could not yet answer, but which he could not forget.

THE LIFE OF THE GAUCHO

In August of 1833 Darwin left the ship again at El Carmen in Patagonia. He set out for Bahia Blanca, and from there to

Buenos Aires, 600 miles in all. He wanted to see the Pampas, the great plains of South America, where tribes of Indians still roamed. He went with a party of gauchos, the Argentinian cowboys. They were strong, tough men, but very polite. Darwin thought they looked as though they could cut your throat and make a bow at the same time.

Crossing the Pampas, Darwin lived the life of the gaucho. By day he and his party rode horseback. At night they slept on the ground with their saddles for pillows. They ate only meat—the meat of the deer, rheas, and armadillos they hunted. After eating, Darwin sat with the gauchos around a fire of bones. Like them, he smoked cigars and drank maté, a kind of herb tea.

The journey took forty days, and Darwin loved every minute of it. He studied the country, its plants, its animals, its birds, collecting and taking notes. Alone, he climbed a mountain 3,500 feet high. He saw rheas, Pampas cats, foul-smelling zorillos, snakes, swans, ducks, cranes, eagles, vultures, and little animals called tuco-tucos. When he returned to Buenos Aires, he was burnt brown by the sun, and looked like a gaucho himself.

Around the end of September, he was again on horseback. He rode 300 miles up the Parana River to Santa Fe. Near the town, on the bank of a river, he made another good haul of fossil bones. For a week he was laid up with a fever, then boarded a little riverboat for the trip back. He found Buenos Aires surrounded by soldiers trying to stage a revolution. He had to use bribery to get himself, his collections, and

Covington out of the city. They rejoined the *Beagle* at Montevideo. Darwin had cases of specimens to pack and ship to England—seeds, plants, snakes, insects, the skins of birds.

Now the *Beagle* continued on its course down the coast of Argentina. Darwin made several trips ashore. At St. Julian Darwin went with Captain Fitzroy and some of the crew to find fresh water. They found none. Fitzroy and one crewman, exhausted from the heat, dropped to the ground. Darwin walked back to the ship to get help, and did not get there until after dark. He had been without rest or water for eleven hours.

He seemed to have become as tough as a gaucho.

QUESTIONS, QUESTIONS. . . .

Sailing around the tip of South America, through the Strait of Magellan, the *Beagle* passed the islands called Tierra del Fuego. Although the name meant Land of Fire, it was a land of ice and snow and glaciers. Great chunks of ice broke off from the cliffs with a noise like the boom of cannon.

And, indeed, the ship seemed to be in a battle. The wind roared and shrieked at it; rain and hail battered it; snow piled up on the deck. For a month, racked and tossed by tremendous waves, the *Beagle* fought the winter storms.

As always when the weather was rough, Darwin was seasick.

He may have been a gaucho on land, but at sea he was no sailor. He could do no work with his specimens. Again he could only lie on his back in his hammock and munch raisins.

Stumbling out on deck for a minute or two, he watched the icebergs floating by. They were huge—as tall as cathedrals, he thought. Many of them carried masses of rock which the glacier had ripped from the earth. Here again was proof of Lyell's theory. Glaciers, earthquakes, volcanoes, the action of wind and rain and the sea—all these had changed the face of the earth.

He felt the sickness rising in him and quickly tottered back inside to his hammock. After a few deep breaths he began to feel better.

Yes, he said to himself, Lyell was right. Not only had the earth changed over the years; it was still changing. Was it possible that the earth's creatures, too, had changed? If so, why had they changed, what had changed them?

His mind leaped to the huge animals whose bones he had dug up, the giant sloths and armadillos. They were so different from the small sloths and armadillos still living—and yet they resembled them, too. What made them so like each other—and so unlike? Could they be related to each other in some way?

Were all living things, from the tiniest insect to the largest elephant, related? Was man also related to the other living creatures? Questions, questions. . . .

Darwin realized that these questions would shock most

people. The answers might be even more shocking. For Christians believed that God had created all living things, and that they remained as He had created them. When man became wicked, God sent a great flood over the earth. Only Noah and his family were allowed to escape, with two of every living creature. When the flood was over, life again spread over the earth. All plants and animals, and man himself, were as God had created them, unchanged and unchanging.

There were a few men who believed otherwise, as far back as the ancient Greeks and Romans. They believed in evolution, which meant that all forms of life were related and had changed over the centuries. One of the few was Charles Darwin's grandfather, Dr. Erasmus Darwin. He wrote a long poem called *Zoonomia*, in which he said that all life may have come from "one living filament." But, like the other evolutionists before him, he was just guessing. He had no proof, no facts. No one, not even Charles, took him seriously.

Lying in his hammock while the ship rocked in the storm, Darwin thought of his first days aboard the *Beagle*. There had been no questions of any kind in his mind. He had known exactly what his future would be. He would have several years of adventure, and then return to England and settle down as a minister. He had known, too, exactly what he believed. He was a Christian, he believed in God and the Bible, and that was that.

Captain Fitzroy, who was an extremely religious man, said he expected that Darwin would prove that the Bible was right.

Darwin agreed. But the longer the voyage went on, the more Darwin wondered. When he tried to discuss his thoughts with Fitzroy, he always got the same reply.

"The Bible!" Fitzroy said. "Let's look at the Bible. If it's in the Bible, it must be so."

Darwin did not dare tell Fitzroy all the questions that were troubling him. Fitzroy would have been deeply shocked. It would seem to him that Darwin wanted to do away with religion, to do away with God.

Darwin had no wish to shock anyone, but he could not help asking those questions, as shocking as they were. Or, rather, the questions seemed to ask themselves, to rise in his mind, crying out for answers.

He had no answers. No, he had no answers—yet. He needed facts, facts, and more facts. He was unsure of many things, but of one thing he was sure. He could never be a minister. He could no longer have a career in the Church. He must spend his life in science, searching for answers.

MOUNTAINS AND THE BENCHUGA BUG

Northward into the Pacific Ocean, along the coast of Chile, sailed the *Beagle*—and still she could not get away from the storms. It was as if the ship brought the storms with her. Not until she reached Valparaiso in July did the weather become fine. The name meant "Valley of Paradise." And, gazing at the white houses shining in the sun, the weary crew felt that the town had been well named.

Beyond the valley lay the towering Andes Mountains. Darwin could hardly wait to climb them. Mountain climbing had become one of his greatest joys. Besides, he was eager to study the geology of this great range, the second highest in the world. Once on land, he again forgot his seasickness. He soon hired two guides and set off with them on muleback.

Higher and higher they went, deeper and deeper into the rocky, rugged mountains. Condors, the vultures that feed on the dead, circled above them. They were waiting for the men to fall and furnish them with a dinner. Darwin had no fear of the condors or the heights. Nor did he fear the cold of the nights, when he had to huddle close to his guides to keep warm.

It was on this trip that he made a startling discovery. High on the mountains he saw fossil seashells, petrified pine trees, and rocks that came from the sea. He knew then that this land had once sunk into the ocean and had been raised up by the movement of the earth. It was more proof that the earth had changed over the centuries.

In six weeks he was back in Valparaiso, but he was in bed for a month with a mysterious illness. It may have been Chagas' Disease, which comes from the bite of the Benchuga bug, which sucks blood. At that time little was known about the disease and, at any rate, he seemed to recover from it. He returned to the ship, ready for further adventures.

EARTHQUAKE AND THE MOUNTAINS AGAIN

As Captain Fitzroy surveyed the coast of Chile, Darwin went ashore to collect specimens. In February of 1835 he was in the town of Valdivia with Covington, his assistant. One afternoon they lay down to rest in the shade of an apple orchard. A sudden gust of wind rustled the trees, and the earth shook beneath them.

"Earthquake!" cried Darwin.

They jumped up, feeling as if the next moment they might fall. The earth, which had seemed so solid, so reliable, could no longer be trusted.

They hurried back to the *Beagle*, which had been shaken by the quake. But there was no serious damage, and they sailed north to Talcahuano. Here the shore was a mass of wreckage. Heaps of rock, trees, broken furniture, and parts of houses were jumbled together. Darwin went on to Concepción with Fitzroy. Every house was in ruins, as was the cathedral. Darwin noticed that the earth had risen a few feet—still more proof that the earth could move and change.

It was late in June when Darwin boarded the *Beagle* at Copiapó. The ship then sailed up the coast to Callao, a small seaport in Peru. There she remained at anchor while Fitzroy went to Lima to look at some charts that would be helpful in his survey.

Darwin was glad to have the chance to rest on board. After his long, hard trips, he enjoyed eating good meals and

sleeping in a cabin instead of on the ground in the open. At the same time, he was anxious to go on. He had left England in 1832, and it was now 1835—he had been away from home for almost four years. Like the other men on the *Beagle*, he was weary of the voyage. He often thought of Shrewsbury, and the more he thought of it the more beautiful it seemed.

Still, he could not hurry the ship along; she would not sail until Fitzroy was back from Lima. He rested, he read, he made notes, he packed up specimens to send to England.

And, while he thought longingly of home, he also thought of the questions that kept haunting him. He had seen that the face of the earth could change. Could plants and animals change, too? Why were there so many different kinds or species? What had made them what they were? How had it happened?

Then Fitzroy returned, and in early September he gave the order to sail. They went northwest, away from the coast of South America. They were bound for the Galapagos, the Enchanted Isles. Darwin had no way of knowing it, but there he would begin to find the answers to his questions.

3 / MYSTERY OF MYSTERIES

THE STRANGE GALAPAGOS

Darwin had seen many strange sights on the voyage of the *Beagle*. He had seen the thick tangled rain forest of Brazil, the vast stretches of the Pampas, the rocky heights of the Andes Mountains. He had seen strange animals, plants, insects, birds. He had seen the land trembling in an earthquake and the sea rearing up in a storm. But never had he seen anything as strange as the Galapagos.

Standing on the deck of the *Beagle*, Darwin watched as they sailed around Chatham Island. The waves beat against a shore of black rock, twisted and tumbled as though by the hand of a giant. Beyond were small volcanic cones like chimney pots. Heat seemed to rise toward the low-hanging sky, as if from underground fires. And over the rocks crawled hundreds of slimy, ugly lizards. Fitzroy, standing beside Darwin, said that this was "the Infernal Regions," another name for hell.

The *Beagle* stayed at the Galapagos for a little more than a month, and Darwin was able to go ashore on most of the islands. On James Island he camped out for a week with a small party of men from the ship. As he went exploring, he realized that man was a stranger here. True, whaling ships stopped from time to time to capture tortoises and get fresh water. And on Charles Island lived two hundred prisoners sent here by Ecuador, which now owned the Galapagos.

But otherwise the islands belonged to the creatures that crept on the ground or flew through the air. They had no fear of people. The birds were so tame he could knock them down with a stick or his hat or the muzzle of his gun. The birds, the lizards, the tortoises, the snakes, the crabs, had all made this their home, and man was an intruder.

Darwin felt that suddenly, without warning, he had stepped into the past. It was not hell that the Galapagos resembled, but the world as it once was; this was how the world must have looked millions of years ago. No wonder the Spaniards had called the Galapagos the Encantadas, or Enchanted Isles! Time had come to a halt here. Time had stood still, as if some witch or wizard had cast an enchantment, a magic spell, over these islands and their inhabitants.

"Here," Darwin said, "both in space and time, we seem to be brought somewhat near to that great fact—that mystery of mysteries—the first appearance of new beings on this earth."

Among the beings on the Galapagos, Darwin could not help

noticing the tortoises. They were huge, weighing as much as five hundred pounds. Darwin was told that the tortoises were deaf, and they paid no attention to him when he walked close behind them. But as soon as he passed one, it would pull in its head and legs under its shell. Giving a deep hiss, it would fall to the ground as if dead.

Sometimes Darwin would hop on the back of a tortoise for a ride. He would rap a few times on the hind part of the shell, and away they would go. The only trouble was that he found it hard to keep his balance.

As Darwin walked about, he kept stepping into the burrows of lizards. He could not help it; the holes the lizards dug were not very deep, and there were many of them. One day he watched a lizard making a burrow. It dug with two feet on one side of its body. When these were tired, it dug with the two feet on the other side. Finally, it was almost entirely buried in the soil.

Reaching out, Darwin pulled it by the tail.

"At this it was greatly astonished," Darwin wrote in his journal, "and soon shuffled up to see what was the matter; and then stared me in the face, as much as to say, 'What made you pull my tail?' "

This lizard was a land lizard. Darwin also found another kind, the marine lizard. The marine lizards never went far from the sea. When they were not sunning themselves on the shore, they swam in the water and ate seaweed. And yet, when Darwin tossed one into the water, it rushed back to land. Again and again he threw it; again and again it raced to land. Darwin

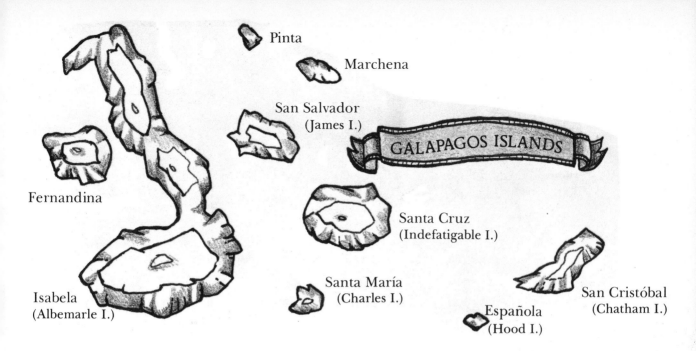

Pinta

Marchena

San Salvador
(James I.)

GALAPAGOS ISLANDS

Fernandina

Santa Cruz
(Indefatigable I.)

Isabela
(Albemarle I.)

Santa María
(Charles I.)

Española
(Hood I.)

San Cristóbal
(Chatham I.)

could think of only one explanation. In the sea were the lizard's enemies, particularly sharks. It had no enemies on land. And so, when it felt in danger, it always made for the land, where it would be safe.

Darwin marveled at the strangeness of the creatures on these islands. But before he left the Galapagos, he discovered something about them even more strange. A man who lived on Charles Island told him that the tortoises on each island were different from those on the other islands. For one thing, their shells were different. They were also somewhat different in size and shape. He could tell at a glance from which island any tortoise came.

Darwin was amazed. He had never dreamed that islands so close to each other—no more than fifty or sixty miles apart—so alike, with the same climate, could have species that were

47

different. He wanted to look around again, to find out more about this remarkable fact, but there was no time. Fitzroy had finished his work here; they must sail on.

Darwin was deeply disappointed.

"This is what happens to travelers," he said. "No sooner do you discover what is most interesting in any one place, than you are hurried from it."

There was nothing he could do about it. He must leave the Enchanted Isles. Gathering up his specimens, he went on board the ship. He did not know that the clue to the secret of the Galapagos, to the mystery of mysteries, was already in his hands.

THE FINCHES OF THE GALAPAGOS

When the *Beagle* set out to sea again, the crew felt they were already on their way home. There were still many miles to go. Fitzroy planned to stop at Tahiti, New Zealand, and Australia. But after that they would be bound for England. The worst of the voyage was behind them.

Darwin, too, felt that he was on the way home. But he did little thinking about Shrewsbury. He was too busy; he had too much to do. As the ship sailed the Pacific, he spent long hours in his cabin. He arranged his specimens, examined them under a microscope, made notes.

Studying them, he felt again the enchantment of the

Galapagos. Most of the species from the islands were new to him. They could be found nowhere else, and were different from the species he had found in South America. And yet in some ways they were like them, too.

"It was most striking," he wrote in his journal, "to be surrounded by new birds, new reptiles, new shells, new insects, new plants, and yet by innumerable trifling details of structure, and even by the tones of voice and plumage of the birds, to have the temperate plains of Patagonia, or the hot dry deserts of Northern Chile, brought vividly before my eyes."

Why? Why were the creatures and plants of the Galapagos and those of South America different and yet alike? Was it possible that in the past the ones on the islands and the ones in South America had belonged to the same species? Had they once been exactly alike, and then changed over the years? The Galapagos were hundreds of miles away from South America, and living conditions were different in the two places. Was that the reason for the change?

And what of the tortoises, which lived on islands so close together? Why were they different from one another?

And then, most interesting and important of all, there were the finches of the Galapagos.

In themselves, the finches were not very interesting birds. Their feathers were not brightly colored; they sang no sweet songs. But, like the tortoises, the finches on each island were different from the finches on the other islands—and the difference was chiefly in their beaks.

Some of the finches had large beaks, some had small. Some had thick beaks, some beaks that were long and thin. Some had straight beaks, some had curved. Altogether, there were thirteen species of finches on the different islands in the Galapagos, each with a different kind of beak.

Darwin looked carefully at his specimens of finches. He thought of the beaks he had seen on other birds. Thick beaks were good for cracking nuts and seeds. Small beaks were good for catching insects. That was it! Each species had a beak that allowed it to eat a different kind of food.

When the finches had first come to the Galapagos, they had all eaten the same kind of food and had the same kind of beaks. Then, settling on the different islands, they had found different kinds of food. Over many years, their beaks had developed into what they were today. Yes, that had to be the explanation—it was the only one that made sense.

Darwin knew that he now had the clue to the "mystery of mysteries." He was on the trail of a great scientific truth, but he told no one his thoughts. He did not even write them down in his journal. To most people, they would seem to mock religion. If species changed, they could not be as the Bible said God had created them.

Besides, there were still many questions he could not answer. Like the earth itself, all living things changed, but just how and why he was not sure. He needed more study. Above all, he needed more facts. And, until he had them, until he was sure that he was right, he would keep his thoughts to himself.

I ABHOR THE SEA

By November of 1835, the *Beagle* had reached Tahiti. Darwin spent ten days there, and wrote to his sister, "The kind simple manners of the half-civilized natives are in harmony with the wild and beautiful scenery. I made a little excursion of three days into the Central Mountains. . . . Yet the woods cannot be compared to the forests of Brazil."

In April the *Beagle* was at the Cocos Islands in the Indian Ocean. Every stop was to Darwin simply one more delay in reaching England and home. He had been on the *Beagle* for more than four years and felt like a prisoner. Whenever he saw a ship bound for England, he wanted to rush aboard. He wrote home that he was sure the scenery of England was ten times more beautiful than any he had seen.

Even so, he had to admit that the Cocos Islands, with their coconut palms and glittering white beaches, were beautiful, too. With Fitzroy he rowed out to a coral reef and examined it closely. From his study of geology, he believed that land could sink as well as rise. Coral islands, he thought, first rose by the action of volcanoes. Then they were covered by coral polyps, and at last sank slowly into the sea.

On the *Beagle* sailed, to Mauritius, where Darwin rode an elephant, to St. Helena, to Ascension Island. Instead of sailing directly to England, Fitzroy touched at South America again. Darwin could not wait to get home.

"I loathe, I abhor the sea, and all ships which sail on it," he said.

At last, on October 2, 1836, the *Beagle* dropped anchor at the port of Falmouth in England. It was a dark, dreary, rainy day, but Darwin did not care. He was home again after being away five years.

HOME AND LONDON

It was early in the morning when Darwin walked into his father's house in Shrewsbury. His father and his sisters were in the dining room. They were just taking their places around the table, which was set for breakfast.

"Good morning!" Darwin called out.

"It's Charles!" his father said.

Nodding and smiling broadly, Darwin strode into the room. His sisters crowded around him, all talking at once.

"What a surprise!" they said. "When did you arrive? Why didn't you let us know you were coming?"

Darwin explained. He had reached Shrewsbury by coach the night before. It had been late, and he hadn't wanted to disturb them. So he had spent the night at an inn—and here he was.

Dr. Darwin looked closely at his son.

"Why, the shape of his head is quite altered," he said.

As soon as he could, Darwin wrote a letter to Josiah Wedgwood. He had never forgotten that, but for Uncle Jos, he might never have sailed on the *Beagle* or seen the Galapagos. Nor had he ever forgotten Emma Wedgwood, his favorite of Uncle Jos's daughters. He soon visited Maer, but he had little time to think of Emma now. He had too much to do—his collections of specimens to put in order, books and papers to write, people to see.

With the help of his old friend Henslow and Charles Lyell, whose book he had read on the *Beagle,* he interested other scientists in the results of the expedition. A number of them, who were specialists in various fields, described his collections in a report which he edited. It was published in five volumes under the title of *Zoology of the Voyage of the "Beagle."* He also began to write his own book on what he had seen on the voyage. He called it *Journal of Researches into the Geology and*

Natural History of the Various Countries Visited by H.M.S. Beagle, but it became known as *The Voyage of the Beagle.*

To better do his work, he moved to London. As busy as he was, he could not put out of his mind what he had seen on the Galapagos. The tortoises . . . the lizards . . . the finches with their different bills. . . . He was certain that all living things changed, but why? How? These questions seemed never to leave his mind, and he began to keep a notebook, to capture any ideas that might come to him.

NATURAL SELECTION

Alone, in his rooms on Great Marlborough Street in London, Darwin puzzled over the problems of evolution. If, over millions of years, the earth's creatures had changed, they were not as they had been created. Had they, in fact, been created at all? No—at least not in the way most people believed.

Millions of years ago, life must have begun in some simple form. Slowly, from this simple form, other forms of life had developed, or evolved. All living things, from the tiniest insect to the largest elephant, were related. All, including man himself, had the same ancestor.

Each species, or particular class of plant or animal, changed as its living conditions changed. An example was the finches of the Galapagos. Those that settled on an island with nuts and seeds developed beaks for eating nuts and seeds. Those that settled on an island with insects developed beaks for eating insects.

At first Darwin could not understand exactly how this happened. He knew that men could breed the kind of animals they wanted, but how did such changes take place in nature? To find out, he met with men who bred horses and cattle and pigeons. He talked to them, listened to them, and learned what they did. A breeder who wanted faster horses would select his fastest horses and mate them. Then he would select the fastest offspring of these horses and mate them. He would keep repeating this, until in time he had a new breed of horses.

Very well. That was how men bred animals. But that still did not answer the question of how it happened in nature.

One day—just for amusement, Darwin said later—he picked up a book by Thomas Malthus. According to Malthus, the number of people in the world was growing faster than the supply of food. They would overrun the world, except that war, disease, and famine kept their numbers down.

Suddenly, as he read, Darwin smiled.

"Of course!" he thought. "Of course!" Here was the answer to the question that had been troubling him.

Life was a struggle, a kind of contest. It was true not just for man, but for all plants and animals. There was only so much food to go around, only so much space in any area. And, in all species, a great many individuals died.

But which died, and which lived? No two individuals were

exactly alike; there were variations in all species. The ones that lived were those most fit to live. They would mate and have offspring. They had been selected to breed, not by men, but by nature. In time, over thousands of years, they would produce a new species. Darwin called this Natural Selection, or the Survival of the Fittest.

As he put it in his own words, " . . . being well prepared to appreciate the struggle for existence which everywhere goes on from long-continued observation of the habits of animals and plants, it at once struck me that under these circumstances favourable variations would tend to be preserved, and unfavourable ones to be destroyed. The result would be the formation of new species."

At last Darwin had a theory to work with, but he mentioned it to no one. Four years later, in 1842, he wrote down his thoughts on evolution in thirty-five pages. He put the pages away in a safe place where no one could see them. He had discovered the secret of the Enchanted Isles, but he was not yet ready to give it to the world. He knew it would shock many people and he wanted to be sure of all his facts.

MARRY—MARRY—MARRY

In London, Darwin came to know a number of scientists. He was most friendly with Charles Lyell, and visited him often. Even so, when he returned to his rooms he felt lonely. He began to think more and more of marriage—and of Emma Wedgwood. On scraps of paper he wrote down his reasons for and against getting married. He was afraid that a family would take up too much of his time and interfere with his work.

Finally he wrote, "Only picture to yourself a nice soft wife on a sofa with a good fire, and books and music perhaps. . . . Marry—Marry—Marry."

Determined to ask Emma to marry him, he arranged to visit the Wedgwoods at Maer. But when he got there, he was afraid to ask.

"No," he thought, "she will never marry me. I am too plain-looking. Besides, she has no interest in science."

Some weeks later, he visited the Wedgwoods again. This time he did ask Emma to marry him. To his surprise, she said yes. Emma had been surprised, too. She and Darwin had been friends for years, and she had begun to think nothing would come of it.

After their marriage, they lived in London. But Darwin did not like city life. London was growing too big; it was smoky, noisy, dirty, and crowded.

And a change had come over Darwin. On the voyage of the *Beagle* he had hiked for miles, he had climbed rugged mountains, he had ridden horseback for hours, he had slept outdoors on the bare ground. He had been able to stand any kind of hardship.

Then, soon after his return to England, he had begun to get attacks of dizziness, of stomach pains, of fast heartbeats. At night he could not sleep, and he was often in pain. The smallest excitement would bring on an attack. Doctors could not help him; they could find no reason for his illness. Perhaps he had picked up Chagas' Disease from the bite of the Benchuga Bug when he was in the Andes Mountains. The doctors simply did not know.

Whatever the cause of his illness, he would never again leave England. He would never again climb a mountain or ride a horse. He could not even go for long walks.

It was one more reason for leaving London, and in 1842 he bought Down House, in the village of Downe. Although it was only sixteen miles from London, it was surrounded by green countryside. And here, far from the Andes, far from the Pampas, far from the Galapagos, he settled down to his work.

4 / THE MONKEY MAN

LIKE CONFESSING A MURDER

The year was 1856. It was twenty years since Darwin had left the *Beagle*, fourteen since he had moved from London. His days at Down House, even Sundays, were almost all alike. He was up early in the morning. He went for a short walk, had breakfast, and worked in his study for about two hours. After that he would lie on a sofa, go through his mail, and do another hour of work. He experimented, studied specimens, made notes.

Sometimes he was interrupted by one of his children. There were seven in Darwin's family; three others had died at an early age. Darwin did not mind the interruptions. He and his children enjoyed each other's company. They did not fear him as he had feared his father.

Once he walked into a room and saw his son Leonard

jumping up and down on a new sofa.

"Oh, Lenny, Lenny," he said quietly, "that's against all rules."

"Then I think you'd better go out of the room," said Lenny, just as quietly.

In the afternoon, Darwin took another short walk. He wrote letters, rested, read newspapers and books. If a book seemed too bulky to handle, he would tear it into two parts. Some days he would get in another hour of work, some days he could not work at all.

In the evening, after dinner, he and Emma played two games of backgammon. Every time he lost he would call out, "Bang your bones!"

When he was tired, as he often was, he would lie down on the sofa. He would smoke a cigarette while Emma or one of his children read aloud. He liked stories with happy endings.

At ten o'clock he went to bed, but his illness kept him from falling asleep. Lying awake for hours, he went over in his mind the problem he had been working on during the day.

He seldom left his house, but his friends came to see him. Among them were Lyell, Joseph Hooker, a noted botanist, and Thomas Huxley, a young biologist. They had long discussions about science. Darwin threw question after question at them, trying to get every bit of information he could.

For he was still collecting facts on evolution and natural selection, and he worked on many things, including an eight-year study of barnacles. No matter what else he was

working on, his mind kept going back to his secret. In 1844 he had again written down his ideas, this time in 230 pages. He showed them to no one but Hooker. To admit he believed that species changed, he said, was "like confessing a murder."

But as the years went by, he spoke more and more openly about his secret to his friends. Both Lyell and Hooker said he must write a book. He must share his secret with the world. If he did not, his brother Erasmus warned, "you'll find someone will have been before you."

So, finally, Darwin sat down to put all his thoughts of evolution on paper. He planned a huge book of 750,000 words. It would take years to complete, of course, but he wanted to explain his ideas thoroughly. He knew they would shock the world. His book would be called an attack on religion and the belief in God, and he wanted to set down all the facts that proved evolution. By 1858 he had written about ten chapters.

Then, in June, as he said, "my plans were overthrown."

TWO PAPERS ON EVOLUTION

It was a letter that overthrew Darwin's plans.

The letter was from Alfred Russel Wallace, a young naturalist who lived in far-off Malaysia. The two men had been writing to each other for some years, and during the past several years Wallace had become interested in evolution.

64

With the letter he had sent an essay. When Darwin finished reading it, he slowly shook his head.

"No," he said.

He could not believe it. Wallace's ideas were almost exactly the same as his. Wallace even used some of the same words . . . natural selection . . . survival of the fittest. . . .

Again Darwin shook his head. For twenty years he had worked on his theory. Were all those years wasted? He wanted credit for what he had done—but Wallace had to be given credit, too.

Darwin asked Lyell and Hooker what he should do.

"Do you not think his having sent me this sketch ties my hands?" he said. "I would far rather burn my whole book than that he or any other man should think I have behaved in a paltry spirit."

"Prepare a short sketch for immediate publication," Lyell and Hooker said.

Darwin would not hear of it.

He said, "Is it honorable for me to do so just because I know that another man has discovered the identical principle? Wallace might very well claim I published only because I wanted to keep the honor all to myself."

It was a bad month for Darwin. His youngest son died of scarlet fever, his daughter Henrietta was ill with diphtheria, and he himself was far from well. Let Lyell and Hooker decide what he should do; he would leave it all to them.

They decided that Darwin and Wallace must both get credit

for what they had done. They sent a short paper by Darwin and Wallace's essay to the Linnean Society, an organization of natural scientists.

Both Darwin and Wallace were satisfied. Wallace knew Darwin had been working on natural selection for many years. He wrote to Darwin that "natural selection is yours and yours alone." Darwin wrote back: "Natural selection is as much yours as mine."

The two papers were read before a meeting of the Linnean Society on July 1, 1858. Darwin did not attend the meeting; he was still in mourning for his son. His secret was out at last, and he waited for the storm of criticism he knew would follow.

To his surprise, there was no storm. The thirty scientists at the meeting listened to the two papers in silence. The subject was too new to them. Not yet did they realize that the ideas they had held for years had been swept away.

TOUGH READING

Yes, thought Darwin, his secret was out at last, he had told the world of his theory. But now he had to give the world the facts that proved his theory. He could no longer spend years on an enormous book. Instead, he worked on a shorter one. The title he chose was *On the Origin of Species by Means of Natural Selection, or the Preservation of Favoured Races in the Struggle for Life*, but the book became known as *On the Origin of Species*.

For thirteen months and ten days he worked, writing every

day. He wrote, rewrote, made corrections. Writing was not easy for him, and he had "an insanely strong wish" to finish his "accursed book." He said it "has cost me so much labor that I almost hate it." In November of 1859, when he held a printed copy in his hand, he said, "Oh, my gracious, it is tough reading."

Tough reading or not, people rushed to buy it. In one day 1,250 copies were sold, and more had to be printed.

At his house in Downe, Darwin again waited for a storm to break. The first letters he received about the book were encouraging. Hooker called it a "glorious book" and said that Lyell was "perfectly enchanted" with it. Huxley said, "Depend upon it, you have earned the lasting gratitude of all thoughtful men." Charles Kingsley, a minister who was the queen's chaplain, wrote that evolution did not deny that there was a God.

Huxley warned Darwin that the storm was yet to come, that he would be bitterly criticized. Huxley was soon proved right. Adam Sedgwick, who had been Darwin's friend at Cambridge, said, "I have read your book with more pain than pleasure." He thought parts of it were "utterly false." John Herschel, a famous astronomer, called natural selection the law of "higgledy-piggledy." The Bishop of Oxford, Dr. Samuel Wilberforce, said, "Darwin claims we are cousins to the vegetable. Shall we insist that turnips are evolving toward men?"

It did not make Darwin feel better to know that Wilberforce

was called "Soapy Sam" because of his smooth manner. He was only one of the many ministers who were attacking Darwin and his theory. Because Darwin said that man was related to the animals, he was called "the monkey man" and "the most dangerous man in England."

Darwin was not really surprised. According to the Bible, God had created Adam and Eve, the first man and woman, and all men and women were descended from them. As for animals and plants, each species had been specially created. Now Darwin's theory seemed to burst upon the world like the explosion of a tremendous bomb, destroying people's most precious beliefs. He seemed to be attacking the Church, religion, the very idea of God.

He realized how strong was the feeling against him. Visiting the British Museum one day, he said to a man he knew, "Good morning, Mr. White—I'm afraid you won't speak to me any more."

"Ah, sir!" said Mr. White. "If you had only stopped with *The Voyage of the Beagle*!"

Darwin's most active defender was Huxley. In his lectures and reviews, he kept fighting for Darwin's ideas. As more and more people read *On the Origin of Species*, more and more took sides. A debate was arranged for a meeting of the British Association for the Advancement of Science, to take place at Oxford University. One of the speakers was to be Bishop Wilberforce, and he let everyone know he intended to "smash Darwin." Huxley and Hooker would speak for Darwin, who did not plan to attend. He was not feeling well. Besides, he knew there would be a battle, and he hated battles.

"I would as soon have died," he said, "as tried to answer the Bishop in such an assembly."

But others on both sides were eager for battle, and Oxford buzzed with excitement.

THE LORD HATH DELIVERED HIM

The meeting began on April 30, 1860, and lasted three days. On the first two days nothing much happened. A number of scientists spoke, almost all against Darwin.

Huxley felt it was useless for him to stay. This was no place for a serious scientific discussion. Most of the scientists present had already made up their minds, and nothing he said would make any difference. Besides, he was tired. He decided to go home. Let someone else answer Wilberforce.

Out on the street, Huxley met Robert Chambers, who also supported Darwin.

When Chambers heard that Huxley was leaving, he said, "You cannot desert us. You must stay."

"Oh!" said Huxley. "If you are going to take it that way, I'll come and have my share of what is going on."

And so, on the third day of the meeting, Huxley sat on the platform with Hooker, Wilberforce, and several others. He watched as people crowded into the hall, more than seven hundred of them. There were scientists, ministers who had come to cheer for Wilberforce, students from the university, and people who wanted to see the fun. The meeting had been moved from a small lecture room to the library. Even so, some of the men had to stand, while the ladies sat on the window ledges.

The crowd hardly listened to the first few speakers. They had come to hear the great debate between Huxley and Wilberforce, and they were bored. They hooted and shouted, and three of the speakers quickly gave up and sat down.

Then a little man who spoke strangely stood up on the platform. He drew a diagram on the blackboard.

"Let this point A be the man," he said, "and this point B be the mawnkey."

"Mawnkey, mawnkey, mawnkey!" shouted the students. The little man sat down, but the students kept chanting: "Mawnkey, mawnkey, mawnkey!"

The chairman called for order. It was some time before he could introduce Bishop Wilberforce.

When the crowd had become completely quiet, Wilberforce began to speak. He was a good speaker, and knew it. Not for nothing was he called Soapy Sam. He made fun of Darwin. He made fun of evolution and natural selection. Why, the whole idea was ridiculous! Each living thing on earth had been specially created by God. Each was exactly as it had been created. Man was man, monkey was monkey. To deny that was to deny God and religion.

71

Again and again, as his words rolled out, cheers and applause filled the hall. Sure that he had won a great victory, sure that the crowd was with him, he turned to Huxley. A slight smile on his face, he delivered his final blow.

"I should like to ask," he said politely, "is it through your grandmother or your grandfather that you claim descent from a monkey?"

And, while the crowd roared with laughter and the ladies waved their handkerchiefs, he sat down.

Huxley had been listening closely to Wilberforce. The Bishop's speech was clever, but he had not really answered Darwin's arguments. And now this insult!

Huxley made up his mind to let the Bishop have it. He said quietly to the gray-haired scientist sitting next to him, "The Lord hath delivered him into my hands."

The old man stared at Huxley as though he had suddenly gone insane. Meanwhile, the crowd was yelling:

"Huxley! Huxley! Huxley! Huxley!"

Huxley rose to his feet. He began by saying, "I am here only in the interests of science."

Going on, he made it clear that the Bishop knew nothing of science and had been talking nonsense. Wilberforce had not been able to disprove any of Darwin's ideas. Huxley pointed out that Darwin did not say that man was directly related to the ape. What Darwin believed was that man and ape had had the same ancestor. Both had evolved from other forms of life, millions of years ago.

74

Finally, Huxley threw back the Bishop's insult. He said he would not be ashamed to have a monkey for an ancestor. But he would be ashamed to be related to a man who had used his great gifts to hide the truth.

Even before Huxley sat down, the hall seemed to explode with noise. Huxley had insulted a man of the Church! Outrageous! Unheard of! The ministers in the crowd called out, "Apologize! Apologize!" The students cheered and clapped and stamped. Scientists leaped up and shouted angrily at one another. One lady fainted and had to be carried out.

In the midst of the uproar, a man stood up and waved a huge Bible over his head. He was Fitzroy, who had been the captain of the *Beagle*. He seemed about to burst with rage.

"Here, here is the truth!" he cried. The Bible was the word of God, so how could it be doubted? Darwin was wrong, wrong! Even years ago, while still on the ship, Darwin had begun to have strange thoughts!

"Oh, if I had only known then," Fitzroy said, "If I had only known. . . ."

The noise drowned out his voice, and he sank back into his seat. After a while, when the uproar had died down, Hooker spoke briefly. He said that Wilberforce could not have read Darwin's book and was ignorant of science.

As Hooker later wrote to Darwin, "Sam was shut up—had not a word to say in reply."

The historic meeting was over.

AN ACCEPTED FACT

Thanks to Huxley, Darwin had won the battle against Bishop Wilberforce. It was not the last battle over evolution. But, within ten years or so, more and more scientists took the side of Darwin. There were even ministers who said that evolution did not do away with religion or belief in God; it was through evolution that God had created the world and all its creatures.

In 1871 Darwin brought out another important book, *The Descent of Man and Selection in Relation to Sex,* which showed man's place in the scheme of evolution. Darwin was surprised at how little excitement it caused. It was not attacked as *On the Origin of Species* had been attacked.

"Evolution is talked about as an accepted fact," Darwin said, "and the descent of man with calmness."

And several years later he was able to say, "Now . . . almost every naturalist admits the great principle of evolution."

What Darwin said was true enough. But not everyone was a scientist, and for years to come there would be people who refused to accept evolution. As late as 1925, the state of Tennessee passed a law forbidding the teaching of evolution in public schools.

In spite of his illness, Darwin lived to the age of seventy-three. He was buried in Westminster Abbey, where the great men of England lie. Attending his funeral were representatives of scientific organizations, not only of England, but also of the United States, Russia, Germany, France, Italy, and Spain.

The mystery he had found in the Galapagos was no longer a mystery, its secret no longer a secret. Charles Darwin had broken the enchantment of the Enchanted Isles and changed the thinking of the world.

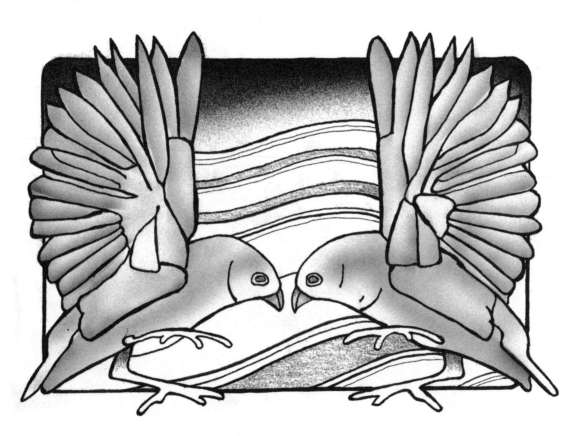

SOME PEOPLE TO KNOW ABOUT

DR. ERASMUS DARWIN (1731-1802)   Charles Darwin's grandfather, a noted physician who wrote poetry on scientific subjects.

ROBERT FITZROY (1805-1865)   Naval officer who commanded the *Beagle*. Later, as chief of the meteorological department of the Board of Trade, he issued storm warnings, which led to regular weather forecasts.

JOHN STEVENS HENSLOW (1796-1861)   Botanist, teacher and friend of Charles Darwin.

JOHN FREDERICK WILLIAM HERSCHEL (1792-1871)   Astronomer and chemist.

JOSEPH DALTON HOOKER (1817-1911)   Botanist who wrote famous works on the plants of various parts of the world.

THOMAS HENRY HUXLEY (1825-1895)   Biologist and writer; loyal supporter of Charles Darwin.

CHARLES LYELL (1797-1875)   Geologist whose great work, *Principles of Geology*, influenced Darwin and the scientific thought of his time.

THOMAS ROBERT MALTHUS (1766-1834)   Economist and sociologist who wrote a pioneer study of population, *An Essay on the Principle of Population*.

ADAM SEDGWICK (1785-1873)   Geologist and friend of Darwin at Cambridge University, who later opposed his theory.

ALFRED RUSSEL WALLACE (1823-1913)   Naturalist and explorer whose theory of evolution was almost exactly the same as Darwin's.

JOSIAH WEDGWOOD (1730-1795)   Founder of the world-famous Wedgwood pottery. His daughter became the mother of Charles Darwin, and his son, who bore the same name, carried on the work of the pottery, which still exists.

SELECTED BIBLIOGRAPHY

Darwin, Charles. *Autobiography, with notes and letters depicting the growth of the "Origin of Species."* New York, Schuman, 1950 (also 1961).
Edited by Francis Darwin, one of Charles Darwin's sons, this contains the short autobiography Darwin wrote for his family.*
Autobiography of Charles Darwin. London, Collins, 1958.
This version, edited by Darwin's granddaughter, Nora Barlow, contains material on Darwin's religious beliefs that was left out of the earlier version.*
The Voyage of the Beagle. New York, Harper, 1959.
Darwin's journal of the voyage, edited by Millicent E. Selsam for the general reader.

Huxley, Julian and Kettlewell, H.B.D. *Charles Darwin and His World.* New York, Viking, 1965.
An excellent short book summing up Darwin's contributions to science and their impact on his world.*

Irvine, William. *Apes, Angels and Victorians.* New York, McGraw-Hill, 1954.
A double biography of Darwin and Thomas Huxley.*

Moore, Ruth. *Man, Time and Fossils.* New York, Knopf, 1963.
The story of evolution, and how the theory was confirmed and modified by scientists who came after Darwin and Wallace.
——and the Editors of Time-Life Books. *Evolution.* New York, Time, 1968.
A concise and not too difficult exposition of the theory of evolution, profusely illustrated.

Moorehead, Alan. *Darwin and the Beagle.* New York, Harper, 1969.
A sprightly and well-researched account of Darwin's voyage, with many fascinating illustrations of the period.

*Books more suited to adult readers.

You can make many more science discoveries.

SCIENCE DISCOVERY BOOKS

MARY'S MONSTER
by Ruth Van Ness Blair/illustrated by Richard Cuffari

"This true story of the discovery of the Ichthyosaurus by 12-year-old Mary Ann Anning in 1811 combines colorful details of life in early 19th century England and interesting facts about fossils and dinosaurs."   —*School Library Journal*

"A compelling book for young scientists, skillfully illustrated."   —*Publishers Weekly*

COILS, MAGNETS, AND RINGS:
Michael Faraday's World
by Nancy Veglahn/illustrated by Christopher Spollen

"Veglahn maintains a high human interest from the very first sentence, without resorting to any extraneous fictionalized episodes but simply by conveying Faraday's own unbounded curiosity and intense absorption in his pursuit of answers."
     —*Kirkus Reviews*

". . . non-technical descriptions of Faraday's work including the coils, magnets, and rings experiment in which he discovered electromagnetic induction . . . . Spollen's bold black-and-white drawings, appearing throughout, supply a portrait of the period."   —*School Library Journal*

Both chosen as Outstanding Science Trade Books by the National Science Teachers Association/Children's Book Council Joint Committee.

LOOK FOR

DR. BEAUMONT AND THE MAN WITH THE HOLE IN HIS STOMACH
by Sam and Beryl Epstein/illustrated by Joseph Scrofani

THE MYSTERIOUS RAYS:
Marie Curie's World
by Nancy Veglahn/illustrated by Victor Juhasz